This Book Belongs to:

For Gail Miller and Andrew Johnson
Their true friendship and goodness
are gifts to the world. —J. W.

For my parents. You made Christmas a magical
time, but also taught me of its true meaning and
the peace and joy that comes with it. —H. L.

Visit us at shadowmountain.com

Library of Congress Cataloging-in-Publication Data

Names: Wright, Jason F., author. | Lyon, Howard, illustrator.
Title: The Christmas doll / Jason F. Wright.
Description: Salt Lake City, Utah : Shadow Mountain, [2019] | Summary: Based on a true story from the life of Gail Saxton Miller, who owned a simple treasured doll as a little girl while living in poverty in the 1940s.
Identifiers: LCCN 2019019685 | ISBN 9781629726113 (hardbound : alk. paper)
Subjects: | CYAC: Dolls—Fiction. | Poverty—Fiction. | Christmas—Fiction. | Miller, Gail—Fiction. | LCGFT: Christmas fiction.
Classification: LCC PZ7.1.W77 Ch 2019 | DDC [E]—dc23
LC record available at https://lccn.loc.gov/2019019685

Printed in China   6/2019
Four Colour Print Group, Nansha, China

10 9 8 7 6 5 4 3 2 1

JASON F. WRIGHT

The Christmas Doll

Based on a true story
from the life of Gail Saxton Miller

Illustrated by **HOWARD LYON**

SHADOW
MOUNTAIN

❧ • 1949 • ❧

Gail sat on the floor of her living room pretending to rub Christmas Eve sleep from her blue eyes. But the little girl in the hand-me-down nightgown couldn't fool her wise mom and dad. They knew none of the Saxton kids had slept much on the most exciting night of the year.

Although she'd collected only one gift from under the tree, it was beautifully wrapped and had her name written on the tag in lettering so lovely it looked like it could have been a present all by itself.

While she waited her turn, Gail cradled the gift in her lap like it was a baby and gently tousled the bow like wispy hair.

F inally!" Gail said when it was her turn. Each member of the family focused on her as if she were opening the greatest gift ever given. Mary, a kind woman who was staying with the Saxtons, also watched from a nearby chair.

"Any guesses?" Gail's mother asked.

Gail shook her head, but she really hadn't heard the question. She was carefully removing the tag and pulling the strips of tape from the wrapping paper, just in case her mother needed to reuse the paper next year.

Gail moved slowly, revealing the box beneath the paper an inch or two at a time.

Then a wide smile fell across her face like snowflakes.

"It's a brand-new doll," she said, but not in a squeal of delight. Instead, she almost whispered the words in her most reverent church voice.

She'd been waiting a long time for something special and new, meant just for her, and not handed down or purchased at the large thrift store down the street.

Are you happy?" her father asked.

Gail looked up at him and answered with happy tears and a smile so bright it could have lit every tree in their neighborhood.

• • •

Gail spent every moment of the holiday break from school with her new doll. She dressed her up, curled her blonde hair, and shared secrets in her tiny ear. The doll was extra special because, unlike any other Gail had ever seen, this one had hair that could be shampooed, dried, and styled.

Soon, winter turned to spring and the two new friends played together outside. They planted flowers and lay in the grass watching clouds race like lambs frolicking across the sky.

When summertime arrived, Gail performed a swing set circus show in the backyard, and Christmas Doll watched and smiled with the rest of the cheering audience.

When school started, the leaves on the apricot trees around the Saxton home began to fall.

As the season's brilliant colors turned from bright to dull, Gail noticed Christmas Doll's pretty features had begun to fade too.

Her friendly eyes were tired.

Her hair was matted and thinning. Her dress was fraying.

The greatest gift Gail had ever received was no longer new. It was used, tattered, and ordinary.

Finally, one cold and quiet evening in November, Gail abandoned
the once cherished gift on a lonely shelf in her bedroom.
She didn't even say goodbye.

Several weeks later, Gail overheard her mother speaking with Mary, the family's houseguest.

"Take the box and do what you can. And thank you, Mary. You are so kind. If this works, it just might be a miracle."

Gail entered the room and found her mother sitting with Mary on the edge of her bed.

Gail spotted a covered cardboard box in Mary's lap.

Mary placed her hand briefly on Mrs. Saxton's, smiled at Gail, and then quietly left the room.

"Is everything all right?" Gail asked when she and her mother were alone.

Mrs. Saxton pulled her daughter in for a long hug and kissed her on the top of her head.

"I hope so," she said.

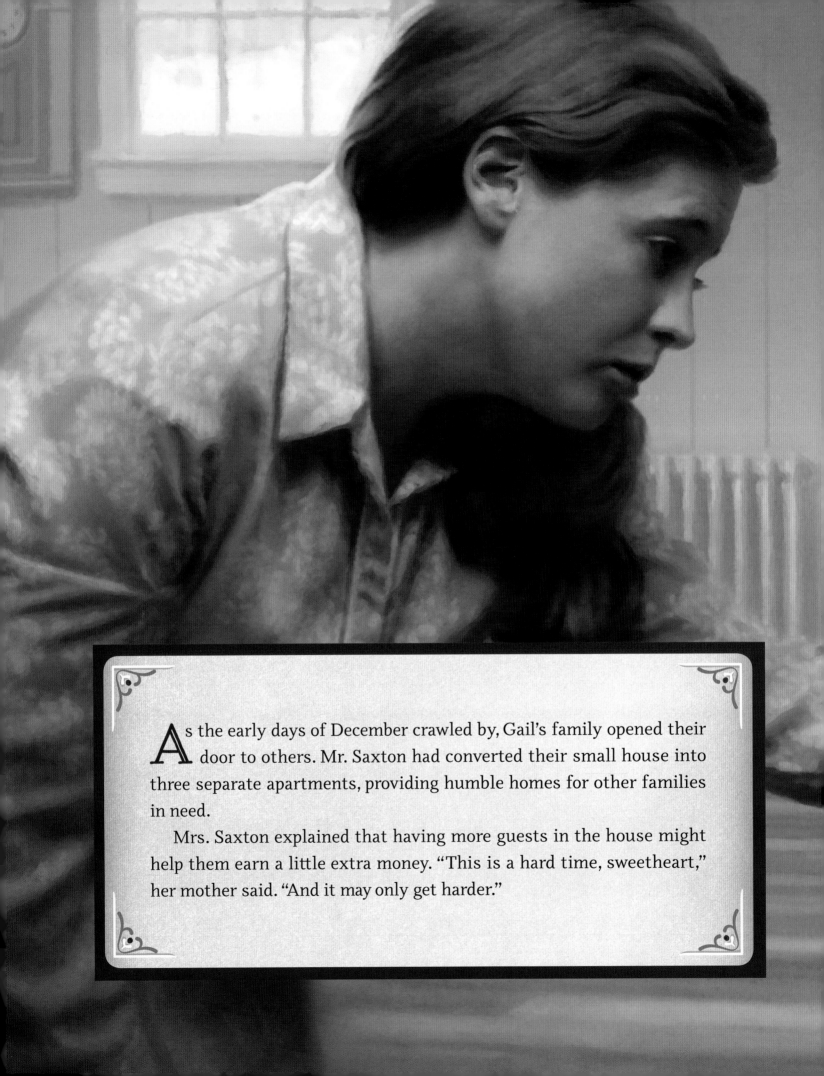

As the early days of December crawled by, Gail's family opened their door to others. Mr. Saxton had converted their small house into three separate apartments, providing humble homes for other families in need.

Mrs. Saxton explained that having more guests in the house might help them earn a little extra money. "This is a hard time, sweetheart," her mother said. "And it may only get harder."

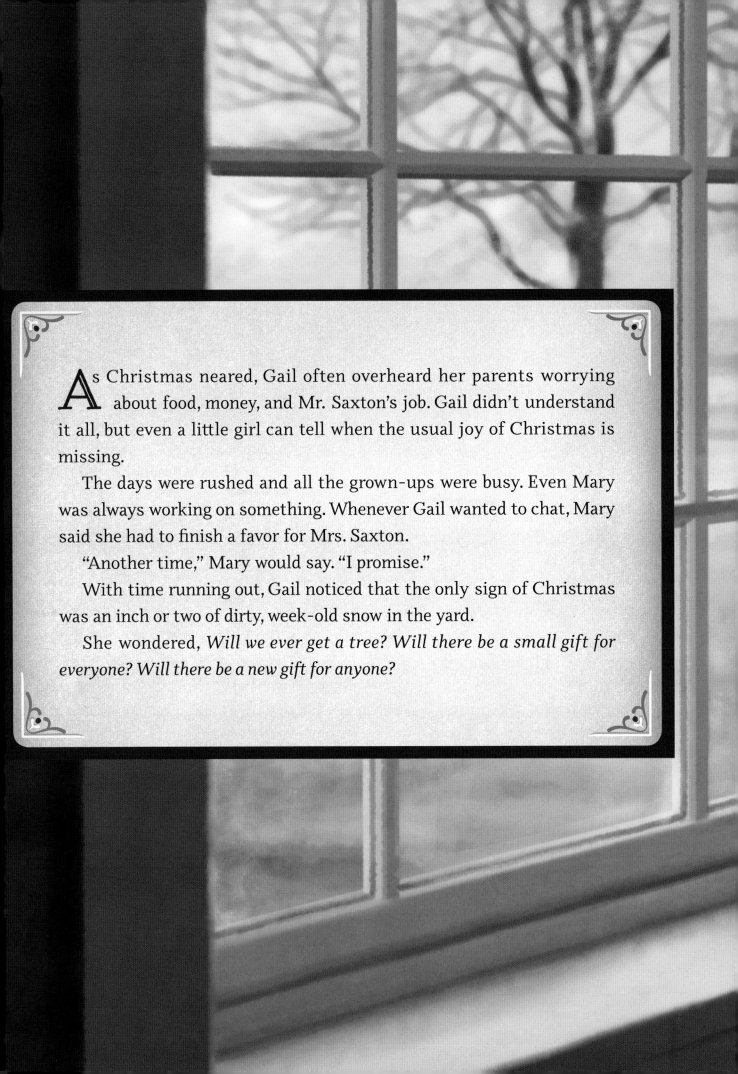

As Christmas neared, Gail often overheard her parents worrying about food, money, and Mr. Saxton's job. Gail didn't understand it all, but even a little girl can tell when the usual joy of Christmas is missing.

The days were rushed and all the grown-ups were busy. Even Mary was always working on something. Whenever Gail wanted to chat, Mary said she had to finish a favor for Mrs. Saxton.

"Another time," Mary would say. "I promise."

With time running out, Gail noticed that the only sign of Christmas was an inch or two of dirty, week-old snow in the yard.

She wondered, *Will we ever get a tree? Will there be a small gift for everyone? Will there be a new gift for anyone?*

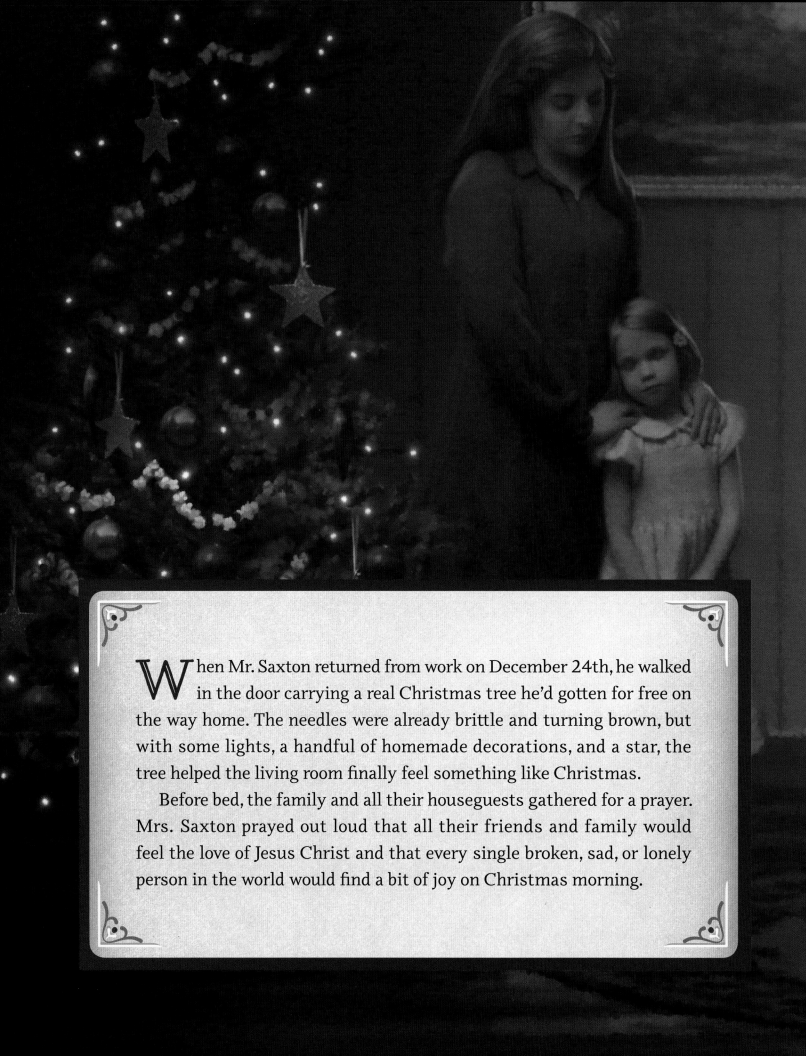

When Mr. Saxton returned from work on December 24th, he walked in the door carrying a real Christmas tree he'd gotten for free on the way home. The needles were already brittle and turning brown, but with some lights, a handful of homemade decorations, and a star, the tree helped the living room finally feel something like Christmas.

Before bed, the family and all their houseguests gathered for a prayer. Mrs. Saxton prayed out loud that all their friends and family would feel the love of Jesus Christ and that every single broken, sad, or lonely person in the world would find a bit of joy on Christmas morning.

Before the sun was up, Gail and her family gathered near the tree. Once again, Gail pretended to rub Christmas Eve sleep from her blue eyes.

Fresh snow and a few small gifts had arrived overnight, and Gail's eyes spotted one with her name again written beautifully on a white tag. She wondered if any gift could ever top the brand-new doll she'd received one year earlier.

At her turn, Gail opened the package carefully. This year, the box was brown and plain with no writing or clues as to what treasure might be hidden inside.

As she pulled open the top, Gail squealed, "She's beautiful! It's another new doll!" She lifted the doll and hugged it tight. It was stylishly dressed, with every single hair perfectly in place.

Gail looked into the bright, happy eyes of her new gift. "She's so perfect. Just like last year. Maybe even better."

Winter melted into spring, then summer, then fall and winter all over again as Gail and her Christmas gift played together like best friends.

. . .

Gail does not recall exactly when she discovered her mother and Mary's secret from that magical Christmas morning so many years ago.

Mary had indeed performed a miracle. She'd taken a tired and weary Christmas Doll and given it new life with a new hand-sewn dress, delicately repaired hair, and repainted features.

As Gail grew, the lesson of the Christmas Doll grew too. Looking deep into the eyes of the gift she had fallen in love with—twice—Gail discovered that just as a simple doll in a cardboard box can become new again, Jesus Christ has the power to make old things new, to heal the broken, and to give second chances.

Through Him, none are abandoned. None are hopeless. All are found. All are restored. Eyes are made bright.
Even Christmas Dolls, the little girls who receive them, and us.

And he that sat upon the throne said,
Behold, I make all things new.

—Revelation 21:5